For my mother, Anne McNeil McLean Love Smith,
who never let me forget that I am one-half foreign—
and who told me I could be whatever I wanted to be.
I miss you. —J. M.

For me and my daughter. —M. S.

Library of Congress Cataloging-in-Publication Data

Moore, Julianne.
My mom is a foreigner, but not to me / by Julianne Moore ; illustrated by Meilo So.
p. cm.
ISBN 978-1-4521-0792-9 (alk. paper)
1. Mothers—Juvenile fiction. 2. Mother and child—Juvenile fiction.
3. Immigrants—United States—Juvenile fiction.
[1. Stories in rhyme. 2. Mothers—Fiction. 3. Mother and child—Fiction.
4. Immigrants—Fiction.] I. So, Meilo, ill. II. Title.
PZ8.3.M78342My 2013
813.54--dc23
2013008426

Manufactured in Great Britain.

Book design by Kristine Brogno.
The illustrations in this book were rendered in watercolor and ink,
gouache and pencils on Saunders Waterford paper.

10 9 8 7 6 5 4 3 2 1

Chronicle Books LLC
680 Second Street, San Francisco, California 94107

Chronicle Books—we see things differently.
Become part of our community at www.chroniclekids.com.

FESTIVALS AND HOLIDAYS ANSWER KEY:
1. CHINESE NEW YEAR **2.** HANUKKAH **3.** CHRISTMAS **4.** ST. NICHOLAS DAY
5. BURNS NIGHT **6.** KWANZAA **7.** EASTER **8.** DAY OF THE DEAD **9.** OTSUKIMI **10.** ST. LUCIA DAY

My Mom

Is a Foreigner, But Not to Me

written by
JULIANNE MOORE

illustrated by
MEILO SO

chronicle books · san francisco

My Mom is a foreigner,
She's from another place.

She came when she was ten years old,
With only one suitcase.

She took a BOAT to get here!

SHE DIDN'T KNOW THE WAY.

She came here with my Opa.
It took them days and days.

She's different than the other Moms
Because she's not from here.
There's lots of stuff about her
That sometimes seems so weird.

zu hause ist es am Schönsten
Fussball
Swimming
Birthdays

Cafe Dolce
Fun Club

She makes me do stuff foreign ways. She says that "it's polite."
I HAVE to tell her all the time that she's not always right.

"I don't HAVE to take my shoes off."

"I WON'T BRING SOUP TO SCHOOL."

"Other kids don't kiss three times, Mom,
I MEAN it, it's not cool!"

Some people say we look alike.
Others wonder: “What’s HER name?”
I get so upset when they say,
“Why don’t you look the same?”

SHE TALKS A LITTLE FUNNY.

She has an accent: it is French!

She had to learn a new language here
Because her words weren't making sense.

She has some funny sayings
That are hard to understand,
Unless you are from Scotland,
Italy, or Japan.

Saturday Morning Fun Club
There is luck in the last helping.

MO
Peti
cho

She calls me foreign nicknames,

WEE ONE,

liebchen,

bebe.

I tell her all the time

"Those words sound so crazy!"

We eat funny kinds of foods sometimes.

I love it.

It tastes GROSS.

My Grandma made it, she taught my Mom.

I PUT IT ON MY TOAST!

You may not understand the clothes
My Mom wears every day.
Sometimes she wears WEIRDER clothes
For special holidays.

My Mom gave me a dress she loved.
She had it when she was small.
I wore it almost every day
Until I got too tall.

She sometimes twists and knots my hair
In strange old-fashioned braids.
I told her she can't do it
Once I'm out of the first grade.

She sings songs in other languages.
I know them all by heart.
I was tiny when I learned them,
And I sing ALL the parts.

We celebrate some holidays on a different day or two,

And sometimes I find PRESENTS stuck inside my SHOE.

I call her "Mom" in public,
But that's not her REAL name.

It's **Mutti,**
Mamma,
Mummy,
MAMAN.

Just "Mom" is not the same.

O! MOM!
Mama!
Maman
Mam

Sometimes it's hard work
Teaching my Mom stuff,
But she's learning more each day.
She'll be done when I'm grown up.

There are SOME things I don't tell her,
Because she already knows,
Like how she should take care of me,
From my head down to my toes.

She teaches me to read.

She sings when I am sad.

SHE LISTENS TO MY STORIES,

And hugs me when I'm mad.

She gives me lots of kisses.

She tucks me in at night.

She laughs at ALL my jokes.

SHE HOLDS ME VERY TIGHT.

She might seem kind of different,
And you'd be right I guess,
But compared to OTHER Moms,
I know that she's the best.

Buona Notte!
Oyasumi, Mama
I LOVE YOU, MOMMY

I love her more than anything,
And you can plainly see
My Mom is a foreigner…

But not to me!